CARTOON NETWORK® SCOOBY-DOO!

THE HAUNTED SKI LODGE

By Gail Herman

Illustrated by Duendes del Sur

WORLDWIDE PUBLISHING ™

SCHOLASTIC INC.

New York Toronto London Auckland Sydney
Mexico City New Delhi Hong Kong Buenos Aires

ISBN 0-439-33493-4

18 17   8/0

Designed by Maria Stasavage
Printed in the U.S.A.
First Scholastic printing, December 2001

"Rrrrr!" "Brrrr!" Scooby-Doo and Shaggy
hugged each other to keep warm.
"Like, it's freezing out here," said Shaggy.
"Well, it is winter," said Velma.
"And we are outside, waiting to ski," Daphne
added.
"And you are eating ice cream," said Fred.

3

Shaggy grinned. "Well, Scoob, old buddy. Let's get some *hot* dogs then!"

Scooby's teeth chattered. "Rummy!"

"Ski lodge, here we come!" said Shaggy.

"Not so fast!" said Fred. "We came to this mountain to ski. And that is what we are going to do."

"But we better do it fast," Velma said. "I heard there is a storm watch. If the snow gets bad, the mountain may close."

Velma, Fred, and Daphne hopped onto the ski lift.

"See you at the top!" said Daphne.

Then it was Shaggy and Scooby's turn.

"Oomph!" The bench crashed into them, and
they tumbled onto the seat.
"Going up!" said Shaggy.
The buddies glided over the trees to the top
of the mountain.

8

"Time to get off, good buddy," Shaggy said. "Count to three, then we jump."

"Rokay," said Scooby. "Ron, roo . . ."

"Ree!" Scooby and Shaggy jumped off the ski lift. "Woooooaaaaah!"
They slipped and slid and teetered and tottered off the path, and away from their friends. They couldn't stop.

Finally, they stumbled to a stop — in front
of another ski lodge.
"How about a rest?" said Shaggy.
"Reah!" said Scooby.
Shaggy grinned. "Groovy. We can get those
hot dogs now!"

Inside, the lodge was dark. Cobwebs hung from the ceiling. Sheets covered tables. And dust covered everything.

"There's no one here," said Shaggy,
disappointed. "No cooks or waiters."
He picked up a phone. "And no dial tone.
We can't even call for pizza."

"Rait!"

Scooby padded through swinging doors, into the kitchen.

He sniffed around the cabinets.

"Rummy!"

"Yummy?" said Shaggy. He opened a door.
Out tumbled popcorn, potato chips, and all
sorts of food and drinks.
"Eat first!" Shaggy shouted. "Ski later!"

Scooby ripped open one bag.
Shaggy ripped open another.
They began to eat.
C-r-e-a-k!
Shaggy stopped in the middle of biting
a chip.
"What was that?"

C-R-E-A-K!

Slowly, slowly, the kitchen door swung open.

Slowly, slowly, the kitchen door swung closed.

"Whoooo!"

A ghostly cry filled the air.

17

Boom! Something crashed upstairs. Shaggy dropped his popcorn. Scooby dropped his chips.

"Rhost!" shouted Scooby.

"Ghost!" shouted Shaggy.

18

Shapes swirled outside the windows.
Bangs echoed through the lodge.
"Whoooo! Whoooo!"
"Like, it's not just one ghost!" Shaggy
moaned. "This place is crawling with ghosts!"

19

They ran for the door.

"Push!" said Shaggy. Scooby pushed. But the door wouldn't open.

"Rull!" Scooby said. Shaggy pulled. But the door still wouldn't open.

"We're trapped!" Shaggy cried.

They crawled under the table.
"Oh, why did we go off on our own?" Shaggy
sobbed. "How are we going to get out?"

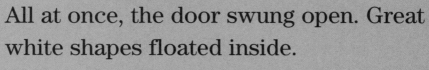

All at once, the door swung open. Great
white shapes floated inside.

"Zoinks! They're closing in!" said Shaggy.

One lifted an arm and pointed right at them.

"Raggy!" shouted Scooby. "Run!"

The buddies raced around the ghosts.
"Stop!" one commanded.
Shaggy skidded to a stop. The voice sounded familiar.
"What are you guys doing?" asked another ghost.
"Are you okay?" asked the third.

"Velma?" said Shaggy. "Fred?"

"Raphne?" Scooby added.

Velma, Daphne, and Fred shook off the snow covering their heads, arms, and legs.

"Of course it's us," said Fred. "We followed your tracks to find you."
"We thought you were ghosts," Shaggy explained, "and that this place is haunted."

Whooooo! Whoooo! Boom! Crash!
Shaggy jumped into Scooby's arms.
"See?" said Shaggy. "Listen to that!"
"The wind is making the whooo noise,"
Velma said.
"And the booms?" asked Shaggy.

"That's just tree branches hitting the roof."
Shaggy pointed to the white shapes outside
the window. "Explain that!"
Fred laughed. "Easy. It's snow blowing
around."

"But the door opened and closed by itself," said Shaggy. "Then it was stuck. This place really is haunted!"

Shaggy tried to run but slipped in a puddle of melted snow.

"Don't be silly," said Velma. "The wind blew against the door so hard, it wouldn't open."

Daphne patted Scooby. "The storm is really bad. The mountain is closing."
Fred checked his watch. "We missed the last ski lift run. What are we going to do now?"

Velma shrugged. "We can build a fire and wait right here."

Scooby gulped. "Rere?"

"This place gives me the creeps, but okay," Shaggy said, and he walked away.

"Raggy!" shouted Scooby.

"Like, cool it, good buddy," said Shaggy. He pointed to the fire. "I'm just getting the marshmallows!"

"See, guys, this ski lodge isn't so bad," said Velma.

"So long as we don't run out of marshmallows, it's cool. Right, Scooby?" Shaggy replied.

"Scooby-Dooby-Doo!"

Dear Parent:

Congratulations! Your child is taking the first steps on an exciting journey. The destination? Independent reading!

STEP INTO READING® will help your child get there. The program offers five steps to reading success. Each step includes fun stories and colorful art. There are also Step into Reading Sticker Books, Step into Reading Math Readers, Step into Reading Phonics Readers, Step into Reading Write-In Readers, and Step into Reading Phonics Boxed Sets—a complete literacy program with something to interest every child.

Learning to Read, Step by Step!

Ready to Read Preschool–Kindergarten
• big type and easy words • rhyme and rhythm • picture clues
For children who know the alphabet and are eager to begin reading.

Reading with Help Preschool–Grade 1
• basic vocabulary • short sentences • simple stories
For children who recognize familiar words and sound out new words with help.

Reading on Your Own Grades 1–3
• engaging characters • easy-to-follow plots • popular topics
For children who are ready to read on their own.

Reading Paragraphs Grades 2–3
• challenging vocabulary • short paragraphs • exciting stories
For newly independent readers who read simple sentences with confidence.

Ready for Chapters Grades 2–4
• chapters • longer paragraphs • full-color art
For children who want to take the plunge into chapter books but still like colorful pictures.

STEP INTO READING® is designed to give every child a successful reading experience. The grade levels are only guides. Children can progress through the steps at their own speed, developing confidence in their reading, no matter what their grade.

Remember, a lifetime love of reading starts with a single step!

For Mom and Dad, and in memory of Joe Orlando
—E.D.
For Victor Paul
—D.S.

To Dad, who always encouraged me to draw
—M.D.

Visit us on the Web!
StepIntoReading.com
www.randomhouse.com/kids

Educators and librarians, for a variety of teaching tools, visit us at
www.randomhouse.com/teachers

ISBN: 978-0-375-86777-4 (trade)
ISBN: 978-0-375-96777-1 (lib. bdg.)

Printed in the United States of America   10 9 8 7

T. REX TROUBLE!

By Dennis "Rocket" Shealy
Illustrated by Erik Doescher,
Mike DeCarlo, and David Tanguay

Random House 🏠 New York

Dinosaur fossils

are on parade.

Lex Luthor has a plan.
He sprays the T. rex
with his super foam.

Foam covers the bones.

The T. rex comes to life!

Lex rides the T. rex.
He makes more dinosaurs
come to life.

The pteranodon flies!

The triceratops stomps!

Flash sees the dinosaurs.

He calls the Super Friends.

The pteranodon
grabs Flash.
Flash cannot get away.

The dinosaurs
scare the people.

Lex takes their money
and valuables.

13

The Super Friends arrive.

Batman says,

"Stop right there!"

Lex orders the dinosaurs to attack.

The dinosaurs charge
at the Super Friends!

Batman lassos

the triceratops.

The dinosaur bucks.

Batman holds on tight!

Green Lantern saves
Flash with a tornado.

Green Lantern sets Flash
safely on the ground.

Superman fights
the T. rex.
Its mouth is
full of sharp teeth!

Superman keeps its jaws
from snapping shut!

Batman sees

a grocery truck.

He has an idea.

Batman steers
the triceratops
into the truck.

Meat and fish
pour out of the truck.

The dinosaurs
run to the food.

The pteranodon and
the T. rex start to eat.

Flash grabs Lex!

Lex's plan has failed.
The Super Friends
have made friends
with the dinosaurs!

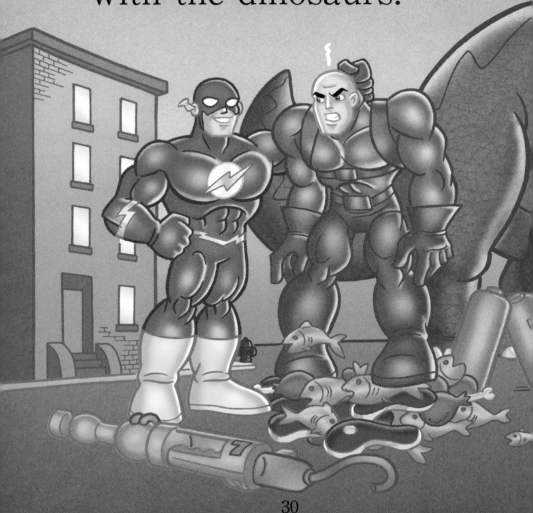

The Super Friends build
a home for the dinosaurs.
Everyone cheers!